Chicago Public Library
W9-BBP-891
monster in Harry's backyard

The Monster in Harry's Backyard

by Karen Gray Ruelle

Holiday House / New York

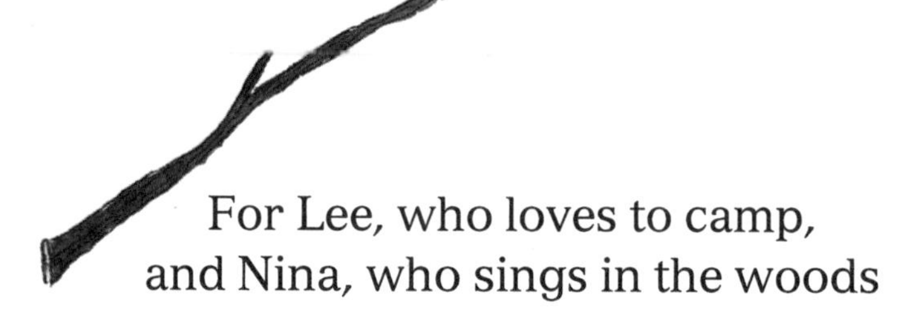

For Lee, who loves to camp,
and Nina, who sings in the woods

Printed in the United States of America
FIRST EDITION
Library of Congress Cataloging-in-Publication Data
Ruelle, Karen Gray.
The Monster in Harry's Backyard / Karen Gray Ruelle.—1st ed.
p. cm.
Summary: Harry is excited about using the tent he got for his birthday to camp in the backyard—until he is alone in the dark.
ISBN 0-8234-1417-5 (reinforced)
[1. Tents—Fiction. 2. Camping—Fiction. 3. Fear of the dark—Fiction. 4. Brothers and sisters—Fiction.] I. Title.
PZ7.R88525Mon 1999 98-17471 CIP AC
[E]—dc21

Contents

1 / The Birthday Tent

Harry got a new tent.
It was for his birthday.
It was green and blue.
Green and blue were
Harry's favorite colors.

The new tent had
a window flap
at one end.
It had a door flap
at the other end.
Both flaps had zippers.
"I can zip out the bugs.
I can zip out the wind.
I can zip out the cold,"
said Harry.

Harry put up the tent
in the living room.
He slept in it every night
for a week.
During the day,
the tent made a great fort.

"Harry, you are such
a good camper," said his mother.
"Why not camp outside tonight?"
Harry was so excited.
He rolled his tent.
He unrolled his tent.
He rolled and unrolled
his sleeping bag, too.

Emily rolled her blanket.

She put it in her knapsack.

"Can I go, too?" she asked.

"No. You are too little," said Harry.

"You will be scared."

Then he packed his knapsack.
He put on his red bandanna.
He hiked to the very edge
of the yard.

2 / Marshmallow Sandwiches

Harry found
a good spot
for his tent.
It was on a thick patch of grass.
It was near a big, shady tree.
He picked up the stones.
He picked up the twigs.
Then he set up his tent.

He made a campfire.

He cooked a hot dog on a stick.

It was tasty.

He toasted a marshmallow

on a stick.

Then he put it

on a graham cracker.

He put a piece of chocolate

on another graham cracker.

He put them together.

te.
on came up.
rushed his teeth
nonade.
ot water.
nzipped the door flap.
into his tent.

He ate seven
marshmallow sandwiches.

After dinner,
Harry looked for frogs.
He found ten little frogs.
He heard more
peeping in the pond.

It was l
The mo
Harry b
with ler
He forg
Harry u
He wen

S
F
H
T

He ate seven
marshmallow sandwiches.

After dinner,
Harry looked for frogs.
He found ten little frogs.
He heard more
peeping in the pond.

Soon it was dark.
Fireflies came out.
Harry tried to catch some.
They looked like tiny stars.

It was late.

The moon came up.

Harry brushed his teeth

with lemonade.

He forgot water.

Harry unzipped the door flap.

He went into his tent.

3 / Scary Noises

Harry turned on his flashlight.
He zipped up the flaps.
He zipped up his sleeping bag.
He held his flashlight.
He held a big stick, just in case.
Harry closed his eyes.
But he could not sleep.
He tossed and turned.
His sleeping bag got tangled up.

10

He heard noises.
He heard bears prowling.
He heard wolves howling.
He heard wildcats yowling.
He heard monsters
crashing through the woods!

Harry jumped

out of his sleeping bag.

He grabbed his big stick.

He unzipped the door flap.

He peered outside.

But he could not see a thing.

It was so dark out.

Suddenly, there was a loud noise.

It came from the bushes.

It was behind the tent.

Harry ran!

Harry ran to a big flowerpot.
He hid behind it.
Then he looked back at his tent.

The door flap moved.
A monster went into
Harry's new tent.

Harry ran to the house.
He ran up to his room.
He was quiet
so the monster
would not hear him.
He shut his door tight.
He hid under his bed.

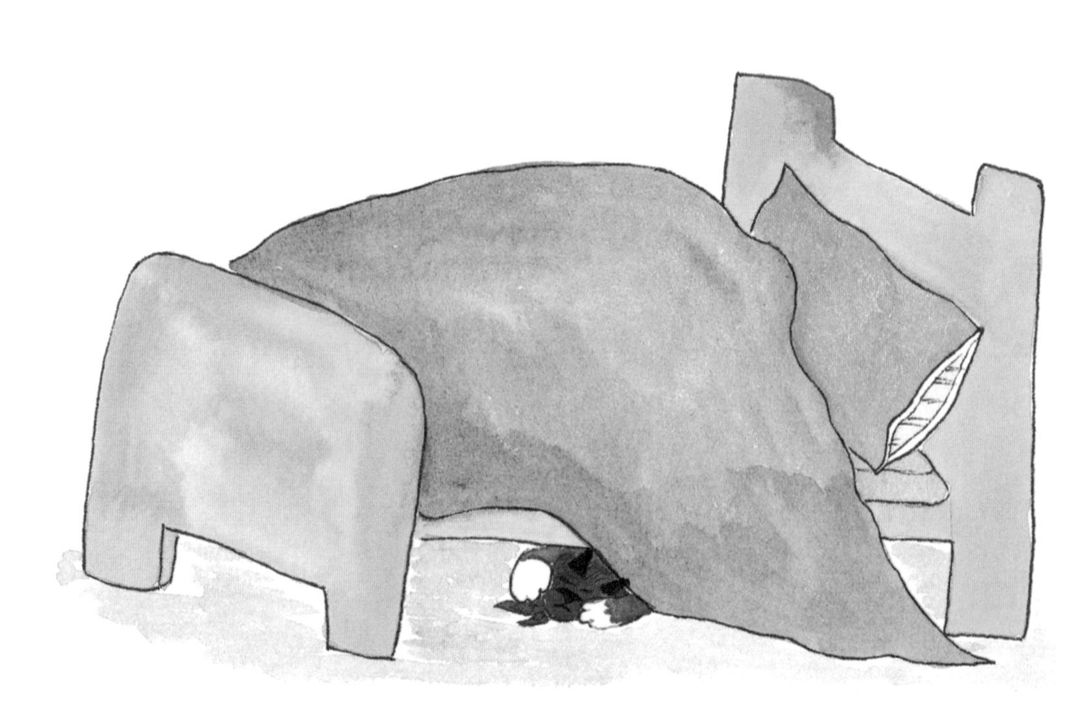

4 / The Chocolate Trail

The next morning,

Harry woke up.

He was still under the bed.

He remembered

about the monster.

But he felt much braver now.

He looked out the window.

There was the tent.

Harry tiptoed down the hall.
His mother and father
were still sleeping.
He went down the stairs.
He went out the back door.

Harry tiptoed to his tent.

A bag was on the ground.

It was a marshmallow bag.

It was empty.

Next to the bag

was a chocolate wrapper.

Harry saw a trail of

chocolate and marshmallow.

He followed it

into the tent.

He looked inside.

There, asleep on his sleeping bag,
was the monster!
"Why, you are nothing
but an old raccoon!" cried Harry.

"Shoo!" he shouted.
The raccoon woke up.
It blinked twice
and bolted out of the tent.

It was full of
Harry's marshmallows.
It was full of
Harry's chocolate.
It waddled off into the bushes.
Harry picked up
the marshmallow bag.
"Next time I camp out,
I will need a helper," said Harry.
"I will need extra marshmallows."

"Extra marshmallows?"
asked Emily.
"For the raccoon," said Harry.
"You can help, Emily," he said.
"You can carry them
in your knapsack."

"How did you like camping out?"
asked Harry's mother.
"It was great!" said Harry.
And he was going to tell her
all about the raccoon.
But his mouth was too full
of waffles
and syrup
and blueberries.